Who Shall Be Happy...?

Trevor Griffiths

WHO SHALL BE HAPPY...? was first produced by Mad Cow Productions in association with The Old Museum Arts Center on November 6, 1995. The performance was directed by Trevor Griffiths. The cast was as follows:

THE PRISONER. . . . . Stanley Townsend
HENRY. . . . . Kulvinder Ghir

Designer . . . . Hayden Griffin
Lighting Design . . . . Aidan Lacey
Original Music . . . . Neil Martin
Producer. . . . . Jackie Doyle
Production Manager . . . . .Simon Magill
Stage Manager . . . . Val Bainbridge
Assistant Designer . . . . .Terry Loane
Scenic Artist . . . . Stuart Marshall
Set Construction . . . . .Guy Barriscale
Technician . . . . .Roger Nicholson
Sound . . . . Green Dolphin Studios
Hair by . . . . .Nicki Gordon at Zakks
Photography. . . . . .Jill Jennings

CHARACTERS

THE PRISONER

HENRY

*(Black up to dark. A distressed grande salle, Palais de Luxembourg, Paris, Germinal in the Year Two; a large metal cage, framing lopsided chaise lounge, chair, lamp within. A slow spot gradually reveals the **PRISONER**, prone on the tilted divan, perhaps asleep, perhaps laid out for burial. His lips begin to move; a soundless struggle for meanings, then a slow disconnected rumble of words. A slowed image large enough to frame the cage appears on the back wall, a late 20th century European cityscape, seen through glass from moving car. The **PRISONER**'s eyes flicker, bobbling on dream.)*

PRISONER. *Who...*

Don't read me lectures on how this tribunal shall proceed, Fouquier-Tinville, I created this bloody Tribunal, dreamed it up...

Who shall...

Vadier sends Danton a message: tell that fat turbot, we'll gut him soon enough...

Who shall be...

Danton answers: Tell Vadier, one step in my direction, I'll cleave his head open, suck his brains out and shit in his empty skull...

Happy...

Vadier meant it. Danton didn't...

Who shall be happy...?

No matter.

Who shall be happy...

*(Prison noises, sudden, resonant: locks, steps, a voice, another. The back-wall cityscape begins a slow fade. The **PRISONER** is up, alert; listens: nothing untoward.*

Approaches the bars. Stares out into the dark. The last of the cityscape seamlessly gives way to a new image, gradually readable as a mirrored reflection of the audience watching from their semi-dark.)

PRISONER. ...Still there? Aye, I see ye. Little white faces in the dark. The future we are hatching here. Fell asleep. Tired. Little white faces in the dark. Waiting to be born. Where was I? Had I reached Paris yet? It doesn't matter. Touch any part you touch the whole...

(A door slams. The **PRISONER** *turns to watch a young guard shuffle awkwardly in, musket on shoulder, Phrygian bonnet rouge, ill-fitting boots, a tray of food in his hands, he spends some time finding nowhere to put it, finally lays it down on the floor, begins to head off. Audience image slowly fades.)*

PRISONER. *(out into the dark; indicating guard)* As you see, we have begun upon experiments... Henry is but the first fruiting. The new citizen, the new man...

*(***HENRY*** has stopped, slowly turned to watch.)*

HENRY. *(finally)* What?

PRISONER. What, did I speak?

HENRY. Don't start that.

(He watches on a moment, clumps off into the dark far reaches of the Salle to gather something.)

PRISONER. I've got him thinking I'm the Madman. Apparently there are two of me. It seems the Committee, fearing a rescue plot, have summoned up a second Danton from a neighbouring asylum and had him caged, identically alone, in the Conciergerie down the road, to confound the plotters. I came in a sealed coach and hooded. Not even the prison governors are allowed to know who it is they hold. But, while it amuses me to play games with this ignorant youth, and might just possibly yield me some advantage, I would not lie to the future. I *am* Danton. It is I who will die this fifth day of April, this sixteenth day of Germinal in the Year Two. True, they like to pretend the trial has not concluded. But we know better. *(He takes out his watch. Studies it.)* So. We have a few hours.

(HENRY returns with card table and stool, lays them down, sets the tray on the table, approaches the cage, gestures the PRISONER away from the gate with his musket, keys it open, fastens a long chain to the bars, beckons the PRISONER forward, snaps the chain onto his ankle, indicates the tray, heads off down the room again.)

PRISONER. The letter...?

HENRY. *(leaving)* Eat.

(The PRISONER ponders, then moves towards the food. Discovers the chain holds him a tantalizing metre or so away from it.)

PRISONER. Who would be an optimist? *(bellowing down room)* What, is the trial ended, and the sentence death by starving, doughface?

(HENRY returns, bowl, razor, metal mirror and towel on a tray in his hands. Sees the problem. Adjusts stool and table.)

HENRY. Stay calm, citizen. That's eighty sous...

(The PRISONER pays him, surveys the meal, sniffs the wine. HENRY takes out a flask from his pocket, places it on the table.)

On the house.

(The PRISONER sniffs it, swigs, swigs again, shakes his head.)

PRISONER. Jesus God. Weasel piss.

HENRY. Spanish brandy. All there is. Have you slept?

PRISONER. I don't know.

(He stuffs food into his mouth without relish. HENRY lights a clay pipe, taps his finger on the water bowl.)

PRISONER. *(seeing the toiletries)* Ah.

HENRY. Fifteen sous.

> (*The* **PRISONER** *counts out coins, inspects tray.*)

PRISONER. Soap?

HENRY. (*from pocket*) Five.

PRISONER. We'll make a rich man of ye yet, boy.

> (*Thumbs razor, sets metal mirror, begins lathering up.* **HENRY** *puffs on his pipe, slyly eyes him, drawn to the man.*)

PRISONER. The letter, Henry. Did ye speak with your Gate Serjeant?

HENRY. I did.

> (*Silence.*)

PRISONER. Yes?

HENRY. He's opened a book.

PRISONER. A book?

HENRY. Aye. a book. On which of us is holding the real You. Us or them down the road.

PRISONER. Has he?

HENRY. He has. An' he has you clear favourite.

PRISONER. The letter, Henry. Do ye have his price?

HENRY. A hundred. That's for him. He says I should ask the same…

PRISONER. He has a reliable carrier, yes?

HENRY. He has a fair few, he's thinking to use the Three o'Clock Runner, he has a set deal worked out wi' most o' the Committee Runners…

PRISONER. Henry, I said reliable, if he runs for the Government he'll be a spy for 'em too…

HENRY. O'course he's a spy, why should that get in his way, he can't live on wages no more than the rest of us.

> (*Long pause. The* **PRISONER** *nods, takes out a draw-purse, lays coins on the table*)

But…

PRISONER. All right. *(taps coin-pile)* His. One hundred. *(removes gold wedding-band)* Yours. Worth three hundred, a year from now five maybe *(takes out a letter, lays it on the table)* But?

HENRY. I've told ye. he thinks ye're 'im. Says it's too risky.

PRISONER. *(lays it out for **HENRY**)* An innocent document, he can read it, read it yourself, Henry...

HENRY. *(looking at it, as if reading)* He says it could be in code, calling for a rising of your followers...

PRISONER. I have no followers, Henry, it's Danton has the followers... He's a huge man, big swaggerbelly, great arse, broken nose, scar on the lip, a Titan, Hero of the Republic written in blood all over him, *that's* your Danton, friend. I'm the former actor detained in a Home for the Temporarily Cracked and currently on loan to the Luxembourg. I'm the Madman.

HENRY. Are you?

PRISONER. *(quietly)* You know I am.

HENRY. I know nothing.

(Silence, eyes, locking.)

PRISONER. I believe you.

HENRY. You could be anyone.

PRISONER. That's what actors *do*, Henry.

HENRY. What?

PRISONER. *Be.* Anyone.

*(Silence. He reaches forward, lays his watch by the ring on **HENRY**'s side.)*

Ye know what that's worth?

HENRY. D'ye know what they'll do if we're found? Carrying letters from Him?

PRISONER. Trust me, Henry. Ye won't be. It's true I have trouble on occasions knowing who I am, I'm always clear about who I'm not. Ye're in no danger. Read.

*(**HENRY** takes the letter, stares hard at it for a long time. The **PRISONER** resumes shaving.)*

HENRY. *(laying it down)* I haven't much reading. Ye'll have to do it.

(The **PRISONER** *smiles at the illogic, gathers the letter.* **HENRY** *walks round the table, to watch over his shoulder.)*

PRISONER. *(reads)* "My dearest wife, I am transferred to the Luxembourg Prison overnight, where I am held in solitary confinement the whole time. Send money and succour post-haste, my condition worsens and I begin to entertain the morbid fear I may never be restored to freedom. Care for my sons, won't ye. I miss them so. And know I shall love you always, on whatever side of the grave. Eternally your Husband."

(He lays the paper down, moves somberly away from the table, moved. **HENRY** *examines it.)*

HENRY. That's it?

PRISONER. That's it.

HENRY. What's this on the back?

PRISONER. *(takes the page)* The back? Ah yes. Post scriptum. I have again petitioned the authorities to allow me to address a company of active citizens of their choosing to judge the condition of my mind and determine the question of my sanity. If ye will, a kind of convocation of my peers... If ye will, a *convention...*

(The back-wall has gradually come alive again, eventually establishes itself as reflected audience. Bleed in stormy sounds of a packed Convention Hall. A bright, stark downspot isolates the **PRISONER**, *as he waits for the presidential gaveling to restore order.)*

PRISONER. *(echoic; intense in the silence)*... Fellow members of the Convention, trusted representatives of the sovereign people, fathers of this proud republic, friends... I do not appear before you because I fear for my neck. If I had feared for my neck, my friends, I should have slipped across a border and saved it. I am here before you because I fear for my country.

And you cannot take your country with you on the soles of your shoes... You will have read by now the contemptible calumnies those terrified midgets of the Committee like to call the charges against me... corruption, malfeasance, conspiracy with foreign plotters, secret links with the monarchists, using the public purse to stuff my own, uncivic lack of Virtue... all the ancient phantasms of rancid and envious minds dumped unevidenced like so much horseshit upon the floor of the Tribunal to steam and stink me to the Block. Well, you'll forgive me for not fouling my hands with it, gentlemen, for in Germinal Year Two, I must tell you, the chasm opened up between charge and crime has come so wide we are in danger, all of us, of falling into the void.

(The hall grows stormy, some clapping, hostile shouts, gaveling. He waits.)

Well then, what is my crime? My crime, gentlemen... *(outbursts, never lost, well up again above the gavel)...* The crime I commit each day I am free is to place love of country above saving my neck...

(Hall acoustic dies. Light from below displaces the downspot. He gazes out at the dark.)

PRISONER. *(internal voice; grave, whispered)* You have given me such a hatred for the present, I find myself longing for the days when the whole of my weekly income depended on a bottle of ink... You have filled me with such fear for the future, I spend my last hours rehearsing what will not happen as though it were already history. So much rising to be said, underneath, so much to hold down, so much to bite back, or choke on. How will I tell you what matters? How will I tell you, as I scan your tiny faces in the gloom, you are yourselves already dead, immured inside the dungeon walls of cant and lies and language this revolution has all the while and under our noses been a-building? How will I tell you I am grown mild? How will I tell you: it is **April**...?

(The spot dies, the salle and cage re-emerge. He sits as before, letter before him. HENRY gazing at it over his shoulder.)

PRISONER. *(reads)* "...a convocation of my peers, if ye will, a convention. But whether the authorities agree or not to such a hearing, do not let Paré neglect Tiger, who needs regular exercise to get his blood running, let him begin tomorrow and every day until I'm home and can do it for myself."

(Silence. The PRISONER dries his face on the towel. Looks up at HENRY.)

PRISONER. Satisfied?

HENRY. *(finger poking envelope)* S'that say?

PRISONER. Mme. Louise Gèly, 22 Rue de Commerce, Cordeliers. My wife.

HENRY. *(poking letter)* S'that say?

PRISONER. Freedom.

HENRY. That?

PRISONER. The grave.

HENRY. Who's Tiger?

PRISONER. The dog.

HENRY. Sounds more like a cat. Tiger.

PRISONER. He's a dog.

HENRY. Does he look like a tiger?

PRISONER. Why would he? He's a dog.

HENRY. Who's Paré?

    (Silence.)

PRISONER. Paré's a servant. Or, in the language of the new political correctitude, 'house assistant'. Now, what could be more innocent? Trust me.

(HENRY gathers the letter in his finger-tips, rounds the card table, lays it down between the coin-pile and ring and watch.)

HENRY. The thing is.

PRISONER. Go on.

HENRY. I've an infirm mother and nine young brothers and sisters to keep fed. If I'm found… Even if you're not Him.

PRISONER. It's a gamble. I see that. *(uncaps flask, takes a pull on it)* The watch is worth six hundred livres, the ring's solid gold. What do they pay you?

HENRY. Three livres a day.

PRISONER. I'd be tempted.

HENRY. Would you?

PRISONER. I would.

HENRY. I am.

PRISONER. You should be.

(He raises the brandy flask, glugs for a moment, suddenly spumes a mouthful of it into the air, showering his upturned face in the downpour. Words form in his throat.)

PRISONER. Germ. Germinate. Germinal. April. Growing weather.

HENRY. *(recoiling; musket ready)* Eh eh eh. Don't start that.

PRISONER. It's out of my hands, friend. It's why I'm detained. Will you do it?

*(**HENRY** picks up the watch, puts it to his ear, smells it. Fingers the letter. Heavy sifting rain has begun outside, drizzling the blue-walled salle with rain-shadow.)*

HENRY. *(delivered as one thought)* I wouldn't get 'em through, there's thirteen doors between here and the Gate House, every one of 'em under special guard for as long as you're held here, I'm searched coming and going, they find this I lose my certificate of civic worthiness at the very least, I paid good bribe money for that, and no certificate no job, I wouldn't get 'em through…

(The **PRISONER** *takes the letter, delicately winds it into a roll, leans carefully forward to place it in the barrel of the guard's musket. Smiles. Speaks as he works.)*

PRISONER. ...Our lives are much like the theatre, Henry, indifferently written and scandalously short of rehearsal. Like poor actors, we must learn to trust one another. And be bold together. Henry...

HENRY. What if they look inside...?

PRISONER. ... They won't. Would *you?*

HENRY. No. But *if.*

PRISONER. Your finger slips on the trigger. Pouf, up in smoke.

(Silence.)

HENRY. If you *are* the Madman...

PRISONER. If?

HENRY. ...how come you have all the answers?

(Silence.)

PRISONER. If I have all the answers, friend, what the fuck am I doing here...? *(He gestures the cage, the prison, the world. Puts his chained foot up on the stool)* Come on, do what ye will, I've had enough...

*(***HENRY*** finds the key, warily releases him, follows as the* **PRISONER** *returns to the cage, begins to relock the door on him, sees the casually palmed bottle from the table in the* **PRISONER***'s hand, gently dispossesses him of it, locks the door. Dwells a moment. Watches the* **PRISONER** *squat in the straw, head in hands, morose, inturned.)*

HENRY. I promise nothing. I'll give it thought.

PRISONER. *(not looking)* Who shall be happy...? *What?* Be happy *what?*

(Silence.)

HENRY. Sleep.

(Clumps to the table, collects musket and tray, stares hard at coins, ring, watch, confronted by them.)

PRISONER. Take. Get the feel of 'em in your pocket.

(**HENRY** *gets the feel of them. Finally pockets them. Heads for the door. Knocks to indicate he's coming through, unlocks it, stands framed in the doorway to be searched, finally bangs the door to. The* **PRISONER***'s head jerks upwards, as the slam echoes around the room. He smiles. Holds up the filched cut-throat, blade a dull glint.*)

PRISONER. I play this game for hope. And know I must hold myself ready for the worst. The *big* one we call the *National* Razor. Sometimes, the Hot Hand.

(*He stares hard at the blade. Folds and pockets it. Town clock sounds the half. Thunder.*)

PRISONER. Tiger? Ye heard me? Tiger's code for the people. As in: if you would master a revolution, first you must learn to ride the Tiger. If the letter's carried, Louise will know what to do. Let the Tiger stir tomorrow, Danton may yet come whole from this. (*Chuckles*) Picture it. A rising at the courtroom, the old Sections armed and marching again, the folk of '89 and '91, the folk of August '92, June '93, the plain people, menu people we call 'em, whose only wish is to be included in the fucking meal… Or in the Square itself, *real* drama, a legendary last-minute snatch from the block… Ah. The very stuff of story-time. (*dwells*) It won't happen. The odds are all the other way. I play this game for hope; without it, what are we if not already dead? In these few years, in this unlikely place, these people have lived and fought and died to claim hope for the human project, to make hope the inalienable right of the living. They have decreed it: to hope is to be human; to hope is to define ourselves as human. Nobody can change that now; it will be so; part of the condition. Like me tonight, you too cannot live but in hope. Liberty may wither, Fraternity evaporate. Equality rot on the vine, Hope's a survivor; and will not die. (*He looks around him: cage, salle, world. Bellows:*) Long live the Free Republic! Long life the men and women who made her! Long live Danton…who did what he could!

(The cries echo round the vast chamber, meld with the sudden rolling thunder, die. He chuckles.)

PRISONER. A world of space to fill with words and not a soul to hear. Never mind. We have our roles and it's enough. Storytime. Where were we? We need some colour, I think, mm? Some people…who d'ye want? I can give ye a whole gallery of folk. You want Marat?

(He muzzes his hair, deranges his shirt, grows short, Italian, scrofulous. operatically intense; utterly transformed.)

Marat you shall have… "Friends, fellow Jacobins. Do not be deceived when they tell you things are better now. Even if there is no poverty to be seen because the poverty's been hidden. Even if you ever got more wages and could afford to buy more of these new and useless goods which industries foist on you and even if it seems to you you've never had so much, that is only the slogan of those who still have much more than you. Do not be taken in when they pat you on the shoulder and say there's no inequality worth speaking of and no more reason to fight, because if you believe them they will be completely in charge in their marble homes and granite banks from which they rob the peoples of the world under the pretence of bringing them enlightment. Watch out, my friends, for as soon as it pleases them they'll be sending you out to protect their gold in wars whose weapons, rapidly developed by servile Science, will become more and more deadly until they can with a flick of the finger tear a million of you to pieces…" *(He stops. Broods.)* Dear Jean-Paul. The Apostle of Liberty, Friend of the People, Seer of the Republic and everybody's favourite lunatic. Met him first in '86, '87, in bed, as it happens, in a rather recherché brothel owned by Orléans, the King's cousin and Prince of the Blood, and run by the Comtesse de

Saint-Amarinthe, I was busy excavating her daughter as I recall, while the Comtesse her mother lay beside us having her motte truffled. By, as it turned out, the aforesaid Friend of the People. Not a lot passed between us on that occasion. I may have introduced myself en passant. I believe Marat may have moaned a time or two, perhaps his name, I'm not sure. Back then he called himself de Mara, a blue blood, full wig, powder, perfume, face paint, breeched and buckled, as befits a man who had quacked himself into a lucrative practice as doctor to the nobility while shafting half the wives of fashionable Paris... Those were the days. *(Silence. He dwells on the man; somber.)* On, on. More colour, more life, more *people.* Who? Say it, say it. Ah...

(He fiddles a wig from his pocket, fastidiously reorganizes his dress, grows eerily priestlike, precise, precious, fashions a nosegay from straw to ward off the stench of humanity.)

Yes, of course... Who else?... Maxim the Incorruptible, Maximillion Miseries... "What is the purpose of the Terror under revolutionary rule? I will tell you. It is to create the Republic. Under revolutionary rule, the public power has the *duty* to defend itself against all the factions that attack it. For it has become clear, midway through Year Two of our Republic, that faction itself is grown the chief threat to our work, faction that fattens on two deviations: weakness and rashness, moderatism and excess. Moderatism which is to moderation as impotence is to chastity..."

(Silence. He stops, tunneled, turned in; eventually removes the wig, barely aware he does it.)

PRISONER. *(little more than whispered)*

The man who has decided I must die.

The man who would be certain.

Who has outlawed doubt. Doubleness.

All blur, haze and hover.

Wrote. One year ago. A day or so

After.

After.

My Gabrielle. Birthing a dead daughter.

Died...

(Silence.)

... And I had.

Detained in Belgium.

Back too late. Dug up

Her corpse

To gaze on her a

Last dead

Time...

(Silence.)

Wrote. A year ago. The same man.

A propos.

(own voice, but the man's wig in his hand)

"I love thee better than ever; and till death. From this moment forward I am thee. Close not thy heart to the words of an affection that shares all thy suffering. Let us weep together for the dear wife you have lost. Embrace thy friend. Robespierre."

(Silence, save for the rain. He shivers, draws up his collar. Takes out the cut-throat. Opens it. Stares at it.)

PRISONER'S VOICE. *(internal voice)* I could never embrace him. Who have hugged hundreds. How do you embrace a vapour, an incorporeal idea...? A system on legs...?

(He rises, carries the blade to the cage door, stoops to work on the lock. Talks as he works.)

PRISONER. Come and speak with me, my "friend till death". I know you're not sleeping, up there in your virtuous cot. I hear you've been sick again. But who hasn't? You'll find me much as I always was, still seeking to extend the range of human possibilities...

(Click. He stops, stands, smiles. Lays a finger's weight on the cage-door. The door truckles a few decisive inches outwards. He fingers it slowly open.)

PRISONER. One road to freedom opened. *(Stares out into the blackness. Lays the blade to his larynx.)* And here's another.

(A rip of lightning, another, across the image. Thunder, close, serious. The back-wall images water seen through trees from moving car.)

PRISONER. *(smelling her near)* Louise...?

*(Bleed in sounds of birds, insects, country; then nearby swimming sounds. The **PRISONER** stares on into the dark. His second wife, sixteen, appears behind his eyes, naked, glistening from the swim.)*

PRISONER. What?

LOUISE. *Wet...*

PRISONER. Yet?

(She gestures him to feel. His hand moves gently up between her spread thighs. The fingers reach her, slowly sink into the black.)

LOUISE. Again.

(She moans, moves on her heels. He lays his face at her lower belly. Her hands draw him in.)

PRISONER. When?

LOUISE. *Now.*

PRISONER. *(desperate)* How?

*(**LOUISE** fades. The tracking shot on the back-wall slows.)*

PRISONER. *(internal voice)* Kissing a son on the mouth. Knowing my mother eats. Horse sweat. Cheesecake and cider at the Procope. Wood-smoke. Swimming in the Seine. My new bride's sweet cunt in my nostrils all day. Frost. Men's laughter. *(a whisper now)* Oh Robespierre, my "friend till death", what will *you* miss, when your turn comes...? The Committee? The Podium? The Terror? The Instruments of Rule? How sad to leave this earth so...untouched by it. How sad the man who has never embraced commonness, who has not dared to be ordinary...

(The slowed bleached back-wall image fades. The **PRISONER** *surveys the salle beyond the cage: rubble, lumber, a shattered chandelier, scraps of earlier meanings. Finds an ancient discomfited wingchair to sit in, a leg missing.)*

PRISONER. *Who...*

The future lies in an alley, its throat slit...

Shall...

Even as we have been new-minting the coins of hope

Be...

We have been yet busier re-issuing the banknotes of despair...

Happy...?

Twin legacies bequeathed on all who come after...

If...

(He gazes out at the dark, trembling at the discovery.)

PRISONER. If. *If.* Who shall be happy if...? *(Cant find the rest. Roars, anguished.)* WHO SHALL BE HAPPY IF *WHAT?* WHAT?

(The roar jags around the space. Thunder.)

PRISONER. *(sings, as he wanders the space)*
A HERO IS HONOURED NO LONGER
THAN IT PAYS TO HAVE HIM ABOUT

WE REAP THE FRUITS OF HIS LABOUR
AND THEN WE SLING HIM OUT.
THIS MAY NOT SEEM FAIR PLAY
BUT THAT'S THE PEOPLE'S WAY
IN A RE RE RE
IN A PUB PUB PUB
IN A RE-A PUB-A REPUBLIC.

(A town clock sounds the quarter.)

PRISONER. The song that toppled a king. We sang that song in August '92, the Champs de Mars again, this time we meant business, this time we would remake the world. Reinvent it. Year One of the Free Republic. Everyone was singing it. There was even a play included it on stage, sung by 'Danton' himself. My friend D'Eglantine wrote some of it, I believe, a group of local actors the rest. The plan was to present it at the next Festival of the Nation... But it fell foul of the authorities. Never actually performed. There was a widespread feeling that the title had something to do with its proscription - "Danton Saves France" - I can't think why. Never mind. There'll be others. *(reprising)*

With a Dan Dan Dan

With a Ton Ton Ton

With a dear old, damned old Danton.

(He wanders a little, begins fiddling at his breech-flap, ends up leaning face forward against the Salle doors. Sounds as of a running tap, as he peers through the door grille.)

PRISONER. Four armed guards snoring like hogs at the foot of the door. *(He pisses on a moment, listening to the snores.)* Historians of a sentimental cast may want to read this as that deep desire in all of us to say "Hello, well met" to those we cannot otherwise touch...

(He looks down towards his feet. The snoring falters, as if disturbed; stalls; pecks on.)

PRISONER. The rest of you will know better. The letter's already history. Ça ira. It's not... (*He returns to the Cage; reenters; stoops to relock the door with the cut-throat.*)... escape I seek. It's rescue. It's not life I ask. It's meaning.

(*He slides the cut-throat inside his leather boot. Finds blood on his neck. Slips on his greatcoat, buttons it to the collar to hide the slice. Lies on the bier-like chaise, crosses arms on chest, eyes closed. The back-wall comes to life: sky, cloud, dreamscape.*)

PRISONER. If. If. Who shall be happy if...

(*Slow fade to black. Town clock strikes: four. Prison noises, faint, approaching. The* **PRISONER** *sleeps. Voices at the door.* **HENRY** *in, rainsoaked, panting for breath. He stands for a moment, checking the* **PRISONER**'s *safe. Fists at the door behind him. He crosses, opens the grille, speaks out.*)

HENRY. ... The prisoner is safe and under watch, Captain.

(*More talk, instructions from the ante-room beyond. From other parts of the huge building, the din of search parties - whistles, bells, dogs, boots - begins to feed in to the Salle.* **HENRY** *lumbers into the Salle, stops at the cage to mutter "Bastard" at the sleeping figure, returns to the table, props his musket, removes his bonnet rouge, revealing shaved, louse-ravaged head. Lays out food-kerchief and cards. The* **PRISONER** *stands, pads over to the bars, watches.*)

PRISONER. (*soft*) Bastard.

HENRY. (*swiveling*) What...? Awake, are ye.

PRISONER. S'the clock?

(**HENRY** *consults the* **PRISONER**'s *watch at his waist.*)

HENRY. (*eventually*) Four. (*lips counting*) Seven after.

(*Turns back to his cards, studies them. Search sounds persist, at distance.*)

PRISONER. What's the commotion?

HENRY. *(untying kerchiefed bundle)* S'nothin'. The usual bollox. The Committee have uncovered another plot. National Guard are sent in to foil it. Hundreds o' the buggers. Ye hungry? I'm havin' me snap while I can. *(He turns, takes in the man's headshake.)* Ye all right? Ye look like death in a dustbin...

(He surveys the snap: black bread, a knot of cheese, a green potato, a pinch or two of oats. Pours a dab of brandy on the oats, works it in, tries it.)

HENRY. A prison rising, they reckon. A Royalist gang under General Dillon, planning to kill the guards, spring the Man-in-question and set him up king or someat. S'what I'm told, anyroad.

PRISONER. Mm. Good to know the Committee's not lost its talent for comedy. So this rising...

HENRY. *(focus on cards)* There's no rising. This place were like a graveyard till they came. Happens a lot. A week or two back, it were a plot to spring old whatsisname and the Commune crowd, none of it ever comes to aught...

PRISONER. Hébert...?

HENRY. Aye, that's him. Gate Serjeant reckons they only do it to keep our toes on the line.

*(He plays on. The **PRISONER** peels back from the bars, sits on the divan, head down, his gaze on the floor between his feet.)*

HENRY. Ye don't ask if I took the letter through.

PRISONER. No.

HENRY. Well I did.

PRISONER. I hoped ye would.

HENRY. Cackin' mesen I were. Thought I'd never mek it to that Gate House. But I did.

*(Silence. The **PRISONER** looks across at **HENRY**, who appears to be deep in the game.)*

PRISONER. And is it sent?

HENRY. Sent? Not yet. It's waiting a carrier.

(Silence.)

PRISONER. I thought ye were to use the Committee's man...

HENRY. The Three o'Clock Runner? Ruled out. He's nailed here till mornin', waiting on the Governor to finish the search and report all's safe. We've had to look elsewhere.

(Silence. The **PRISONER***'s head goes down again.* **HENRY** *stands, lights his pipe, ambles over to the Cage.)*

HENRY. It'll be took. Hard part's behind us. I've a cousin works in the kitchens, he's off at five and ready to carry it... Asks a hundred, he'll settle for half.

(The **PRISONER** *looks up at him, eyes sunk, face pale, drawn.)*

PRISONER. Ye took the purse, Henry, that's all I had.

HENRY. Mm. No valuables, pieces? *(The man shakes his head.)* What's the coat worth?

PRISONER. The coat?

HENRY. *(studying it)* He'd tek the coat.

(Long silence.)

HENRY. I shall need to send word 'fore five. To say if he's to tek the letter or not...

(The **PRISONER***'s hand moves up to the collar-buttons.)*

HENRY. Keep it on. Do later.

*(***HENRY** *watches on a moment, drawn but wary. The man stares on at the floor.* **HENRY** *ambles back to the table, angles his seat to take in the cage, relights his pipe, returns to his cards.)*

PRISONER. *(from nowhere)* I was with my wife earlier. I way lying with Gabrielle, the night the first-born died. But it was she was the quick one, me the dead. Yet I could smell her tears on the pillow. The lavender she kept beneath.

HENRY. Dreams be weird.

(The man produces a fipple-flute. Plays Ça ira, *low, slow, perfect.* **HENRY** *listens, wholly drawn. He finishes. Stares at the flute, his fingers hovering over the stops.)*

HENRY. Will ye come out for a spell?

PRISONER. *(slowly)* If ye like.

HENRY. Ye calm?

PRISONER. Aye.

HENRY. *(the chain)* Put that on. I've a bottle somewhere.

(He heads down the room, finds his knapsack, draws a bottle of wine from it, finds a couple of battered tin cups, returns to the table, crosses to unlock the Cage door. The **PRISONER** *waits, chain at ankle,* **HENRY** *checks it's secured, lets him through to the table.)*

HENRY. Here. *(a mug)* We'll tek a drink.

(He fills the mugs with red. They look at each other.)

HENRY. The Republic.

PRISONER. The Republic.

(They clank, drink, eye each other again as the cups come down.)

HENRY. *(decking cards)* Cards 'r chat?

PRISONER. *(deliberate)* I'm without money, Henry.

HENRY. *(cards away)* Oh aye. Chat then.

(Silence. Wine. Distant sounds of search. They look at each other across the smoke and gleam of the guard's lamp.)

HENRY. Ye wanna play Last Words?

PRISONER. Last Words of the Blessed Martyrs? By the cankered cock of Christ the Worker, child, why can we not just sit?

HENRY. This un's just called Last Words. It can be anybody, not just martyrs. And ye don't 'ave to know what they said, y'ave to mek it up. Wanna play?

PRISONER. *How,* for God's sake. If there's no true or false, there's no way of scoring...

HENRY. Ye get a point for a laugh. Or a shiver. Or a tear. We made it up at school. Them as couldn't read.

(*The* **PRISONER** *stares at him; loves his innocence.*)

Like, you give me Joan of Arc, I say now ye see me, now ye don't, that's one I made up earlier, it's not usually that fast… You say the King of England, I say… (*He lifts a buttock, issues a great mouth-fart.*) That's another one…

(*Silence. A slow, contained mute laugh begins to build up in the* **PRISONER**'s *chest. Splashes of it spray up his frame, to throat, to voice, mouth.* **HENRY** *follows, chuckles, pleased. As the laugh reaches the face, it begins a slow agonising collapse into pain and fear and abject misery. Small sounds move about the jaw and mouth; big in the silence.* **HENRY** *waits, watches, trying to read how things are; where. The spasm ends. The* **PRISONER** *sits on, as if somewhere else.* **HENRY** *pushes the bottle down the table. Touches the man's elbow with it, coaxing him back. The man sees the bottle, fills up, drinks.*)

HENRY. Where there's life, eh?

PRISONER. Aye.

(*The* **PRISONER** *stands, studies the room, as if seeing it for the first time.*)

PRISONER. I'll sleep, I think.

HENRY. Finish your cup. I'll tell ye a story.

(*The* **PRISONER** *sits.*)

Will I?

(*The* **PRISONER** *shrugs.*)

It's not a story as such, it's someat 'appened earlier on at t'Gate House, ye might have a thought or two on it when it's told… Tek your mind off things?

(*The* **PRISONER** *shrugs.* **HENRY** *restocks his pipe bowl, tops up his cup.*)

HENRY. Ye'll recall I spoke of the Three o'Clock Runner, he was to be the carrier for your…? (*takes the man's nod*) Now, when I get to the Gate House with the letter in my musket, my guts are in a turmoil, I wasn't ticklin' ye, I have to hot heel it to the Necessary or my trousers'll tek the lot... Now, while I'm in there, who's in the next box but Birdie, the Three o'Clock Runner...that's what we call him, Birdie...he has this great... NOSE stickin' out of his face like a... tap, like a... *(searches; doesn't find it)* Bit of a jack-the-lad, oh yes, knows everythin', misses naught, meks his way... So we're squattin' there next each other, he's just brought the letter in from the Committee - the plot, right? he's cursin' an' bubblin' he's gonna lose private trade because of it, ructions and alarums are the buggeration o' folks like us, he says... So he's lookin' to make up his losses by laying a decent dollop with the Serjeant on who's holding the Big Un...the Man-in-Question, see. An' o' course he's pressing me for clues, I mean he's asking how ye look, how ye talk, what ye say, what ye wear... Cos he *knows*, he's been in the same room as the Man many a time, recent as yesterday he reckons, down at the Court...

(Silence. **HENRY** *relights pipe. The* **PRISONER** *sips more wine.)*

PRISONER. So. Did ye tell him?

HENRY. Tell him? *(emphatic)* No.

(faint, pre-dawn birdsong: blackbird)

HENRY. Dull I may be, I'm no fool. He's a starling is Birdie. Chatchatchat. He'd clean the Gate Serjeant out and brag how he did it all across town, can't help it, chatchatchat... Serjeant gets to know an' I'm *brawn*, mister. Not a man to *cross*, our Gate Serjeant.

(Silence. **HENRY** *broods. The* **PRISONER** *takes a look. Stands again.)*

PRISONER. Is it over?

HENRY. What?

PRISONER. The story.

HENRY. Nearly. There's a bit more.

(The **PRISONER** *sits. Search sounds drift in: shouts, barks.)*

HENRY. I cross the yard back to the Gate House. National Guard're still pourin' in, droves of 'em, tryin'a form ranks in two hands o' water, the Under-Governor's out, helpin' the officers with the list o' suspects, it's time I were back at me post, I say, better safe than sorry... I'm passing through the Gate House, on my way back, big old stable it were once, I see this feller at the other end warming his arse at t'stove an' holding forth to the Gateman, I say I know that feller, I come a bit closer, I see it's the Three o'Clock Runner. *(long hold)* An' that's very strange, because...when he first caught me eye I'd been minded o' someone else altogether.

PRISONER. *(slow)* Ye lose me, lad.

HENRY. Hold on. Ye'll catch up. Now I could *hear*. I knew at once what were goin' on, he were tellin' a *story*, see, an' every now an' then he'd...do...be...someone in the story, someone else. Remember, ye said it yesen earlier on, 'bout acting, *bein' anyone*, remember?

(The **PRISONER** *flicks a look, eyes hooded.)*

He was tellin' 'em about bein' down at the Tribunal building yesterday, waitin' on a package or someat... and poppin' in to t'Court Room to watch 'Trial... So like he's the Judge one minute, then he's the Prosecutor, he's a defendant, he's someone in t'crowd callin' someat... Now ye see him, now ye don't, eh?... *(grins)* Then he's back to t'first feller. The one as took my eye. And it's Danton. The Man himself. *(He stands, swells a little, going for the gesture)* An' he's *goin'* at the fuckers, like a bull, head down an' both horns shinin'... "Call this *justice*, ye dribbling sack o'snot, ye festering pot o'pig's piss, just remember, those who drink the people's blood die of it... You call my witnesses, all seventeen of 'em, for tomorrow, or this pantomime can continue without me, I refuse my consent..."

(He resumes his stool, looks across at the **PRISONER**.*)*

HENRY. ...Birdie's better than me, o'course...

PRISONER. *(a nod)* Do more. What else did he say?

HENRY. What else? I don't know. I had to bring mysen back 'ere 'fore the searching parties set up. *(Thinks)* Wasn't what he *said* as mattered. It were who he were...bein', when he said it...

PRISONER. *(slow)* I thought ye said he was...being Danton, am I wrong...?

HENRY. *(looking at him)* Danton. Right.

(Silence.)

PRISONER. Well. However long ye live, Henry, it's unlikely ye'll ever get closer to the Man. Poor sod.

(He stands, drinks up, waits, wanders to the cage, sits on the divan, stares back at the watching **HENRY**. *Shakes the chain on his ankle.)*

PRISONER. If ye've a minute, friend...

(Begins removing his greatcoat. **HENRY** *slings his musket, approaches with his keys. Stoops to unshackle him. The* **PRISONER** *looks down at the stooped, vulnerable Guard: sees the head of the cut-throat stuffed into the boot-top; casually removes it.)*

HENRY. Thing is. It wasn't... Danton... I was minded of. Because. I don't know Danton, never met, never seen him... It wasn't Danton Birdie was...bein'. Couldn'ta bin, could it, not for me.

(The town clock strikes the half.)

PRISONER. *(handing him the coat)* Here. Ye'll not forget to send word to your cousin...

HENRY. *(simply)* It was you. Everything. Voice and. Walk and head and... Everything. *(He stands, folds the coat for carrying, drags the chain to the doorway, lays it down.)* I tell ye, I'd never play Last Words wi' the Three o'Clock Runner. He can make ye shiver... Anyroad. That's the story. *(turns, looks at him)* Any thoughts? Now it's told.

PRISONER. *(still)* Henry. Leave me be.

(He drags his legs onto the litter, lies back, closes his eyes.)

PRISONER. *(quiet, metallic)* I cannot speak on this. Too. Painful. Too. Riving. It will make me weep again. And my tears will drown the world. Do not ask. I've cracked enough. More and I will break.

*(**HENRY** waits. Closes door.)*

HENRY. I hear ye. *(thinks)* Mister, I've tried to be honest with ye, I'll not alter now... I'll not let my cousin take that letter, not from Him...you. *(He turns the key in the lock.)* Not now I know what I know.

*(He holds on a moment or two, turns to clump back to the table. The **PRISONER** remains motionless.)*

HENRY. There it is.

PRISONER. *(sudden, perfect)* Call this justice, ye dribbling sack o' snot, ye festering pot o' pig's piss, just remember, those who drink the people's blood die of it.

*(**HENRY**'s resumed his seat at the table, his back once more to the cage, begun laying out cards; glances back at the motionless man; resumes his play.)*

PRISONER. *(internal voice)* There be times we must strut and stamp and shake our whores' heads, though dignity and self-esteem deem it beneath us...I will turn this boy, I will not let him be the death of me, I will win him to my purpose, I will turn him, he will not immure me inside the Bastille of his ignorance, I will touch his soul, he will turn...

*(The **PRISONER** sits up sharply, feet to floor. Glares hard at the young Guard's back. Stands. Shifts to better light. Finds the declamatory stance. Launches.)*

PRISONER. *(sudden, big; as actor)*... Citizens, patriots, builders and shakers of the world's good morrow, you are welcome here. The New Theatre for the Old Cordeliers is proud and privileged to offer you this evening an entirely novel piece - the work principally of the celebrated revolutionary and poet Fabre d'Eglantine, with additional scenes by members of the Company *(indicates them behind him)*, which we respectfully entitle *Danton Saves France*... There falls to me, dear friends, the enduring honour, the impossible task, of seeking to fill the boots of our eponymous hero... Yes, my friends, like a small boy reaching for the Pole Star, I must essay for the evening...the Man Himself *(shifts voice)* Applause applause applause, company leave stage left, climb onto the rostrum *(steps up onto divan)*, find the light... *(as Danton again)* Greetings, friends. Name's Danton, for those who don't know me. Born and reared in the country, the Champagne, but not the sleek rolling part, the scrawny bit...of common stock, decent honest toilers, living useful lives in uncelebrated places, dying obscurely as if they had never lived... So expect no charms and graces, I am as I come... But come, friends, come and see for yourselves. To my village, to our plain family house, to our life some thirty years and several millennia ago, in the reign of the fifteenth Louis - Louis the Penultimate, as I prefer to call him - when the world and I were young...

(He's slowed to a halt, confronting the scale of the problem. Stares at **HENRY**, *who has turned to watch him on the arrival of Danton; moves to the bars.)*

PRISONER. How will I fetch you to understanding, friend? Henry... Why do you imagine the Committee had *me* put here this night? D'ye think any piece of meat would have served? I *played* him, Henry. In a *play*. For weeks and months I followed him, watched him, heard him...studied how I might become him, the voice and walk and head. Everything. *(stops)* So hard to speak of. So hard to...

(Stops. **HENRY** *turns, looks at him.)*

When you stand. In another man's boots. Until they seem your own. And your own. No longer fit you...

Do ye understand any of this, Henry? Ye know what ye know but ye do not know the *truth* and I am powerless to tell ye because my mouth and throat are so...filled by it I cannot breathe, it is drowning me...

(He takes out the cut-throat, grabs **HENRY** *through the bars, lays the blade to his neck.)*

Henry, were I indeed the Man-in-Question, the Hero of the Republic, the Champion of the Oppressed, the Saviour of the Nation, the Towering Titan of the Revolution, the People's Voice, the Bull among men, the Fathering Spirit of all the Republics yet to be born into peace and justice and freedom and plenty, were I *that* Man, Henry, surely by now I would have slit your insignificant throat and fed you to the rats.

(Silence. **HENRY** *sweats, face white)*

Instead...

(He draws open his collars, baring the blooded neck. **HENRY** *stares, eyes unblinking.)*

I'll not be free until He's dead and gone. But may not kill Him without I kill myself. Only in death is there freedom: this is the true madness of our time. *(Pause.)* I'm not the Prince, Henry. I'm the frog who swallowed him...

(He releases him, folds the cut-throat, stoops, lays it gently down outside the Cage. Draws away from the bars, to give the Guard safe space.)

PRISONER. I could not harm ye. For you are a good man.

*(***HENRY*** *stares at the cut-throat, moves to gather it up; looks up at him from the stoop. The man's eyes are raw, desperate. Silence. A sudden loud banging at the doors.* **HENRY** *stands, listens. It stops briefly.)*

PRISONER. Henry...

(The banging sets up again. **HENRY** *collects his musket, slogs off down the room. The* **PRISONER** *follows his progress through the side-bars; sees him slide open the*

grille-cover to mutter with someone outside; turns; stares out into the dark.)

PRISONER. In one month last winter, eight hundred people died of hunger and cold in the district of St. Antoine. In all there are forty eight such districts in the capital. Preponderantly the listed dead were menu people, this sad dullard's kind of people. No lawyers died, no bankers, no financiers and speculators, no surveyors and stock-agents, no judges, journalists, restaurateurs, commodity dealers, generals, elected members of the Convention; in short, none of our kind of people. I ate well last winter. My fire never lacked wood, my table meat, my linen laundering, my horses exercise. Who shall be happy...? If...? *(He's close but still it eludes him. He feels for it.)*... Two summers back, in the rising I commanded from my room that overthrew King Louis the Last and changed our world into yours, better than three hundred gave up their lives that it might be so. Harness-makers, hairdressers, house-painters, carpenters, joiners, hatters, tailors, locksmiths, bootmakers, domestics, laundrymen, brickworkers, staymakers, waiters and scores upon scores of citizens 'below' these whom we in our wisdom had deemed too insignificant, that is too poor, to have the vote. Including two women from the market in Les Halles. All, once again, our Henry's kind of people. Who shall be happy...? Who?... For three whole years, we have been at war, with others and with ourselves. Who does the fighting, who does the dying? Robespierre? St. Just? Danton?

(He stops abruptly. Slowly turns. HENRY's back, stands the other side of the bars watching him, dealing with it all. Silence.)

HENRY. *(finally)* It's the Serjeant's boy down from the Gate House. They wait my word. On the letter.

PRISONER. *(quiet)* What did ye tell him?

HENRY. I told him to wait till I had answer. Ye didn't weep.

PRISONER. Weep?

HENRY. Ye said if ye told the story it'd mek ye weep. Ye didn't weep.

> *(Silence. They gaze at each other through the bars. Birdsong; a touch stronger, heading for sunrise. Soundlessly, barely perceptibly, in real time, the eyes begin to fill, brim and spill.)*

HENRY. *(blinking)* I told him to wait. Till I had answer.

> *(The tears grease the man's cheeks, nose, lips. More birdsong. The room has gradually lightened a little: all but dawn. **HENRY** heads once more for the doors. The man turns away, rests the back of his head on the bars, weeping still.)*

PRISONER. *(internal voice)* I touched him. I know it. He's touched.

> *(**HENRY** returns to the table. Broods. Flicks a look at the Cage. Begins to spread the greatcoat on the floor. The **PRISONER**'s sunk to his haunches in the straw, his back against the side bars.)*

HENRY. *(eventually; a touch annoyed)* It's sent. Go to sleep.

> *(The man sits on like a stone. **HENRY** lies on the greatcoat, stares at the Cage; finally shucks over on to his other side; lost. The salle, the cage, the still men. The dark continues to thin. Birdsong; a blackbird. The **PRISONER** reaches out a kerchief, begins wiping his face.)*

PRISONER. *(a mumble)* My last blackbird. Little fucker.

> *(Bring up fipple-flute and kettle-drum; Ça Ira, dreamlike. Bleed in, back-wall, slowed shot of light on water. Drum, flute, slowed light on water: dreamscape.)*

PRISONER. *(dream-voice)*... Fêtes, pageants, plays, children's stories, public buildings, costume, modes of address, the names of seasons, years, months and days, songs, tunes, dances, custom, practice, ritual... We must create an Empire of Images. All will be re-made. We must colonize not just the minds...but the very lives of the people. All will be remade... A new vocabulary for a new world order...

At Nantes

A clear crisp morning

Two hundred men women little ones

Bound blindfold

In a flatbottom boat

Poled to the middle of the Loire estuary

And scuttled

Without warning

Without due process

Political opponents

Men women little ones

Now enemies of the people

Appear in the new vocabulary

Of the Marat Company who did it as

Vertical deportations

When I said. One year ago. When we were young. "Let the *government* take terrible measures, so that the *people* may not have to take them themselves"... Is this what I had in mind?... Is it? The Marat Company? Obeying orders? The Empire of Images. Virtue and Terror. Hope, despair. Love, hate. Kind, vicious. Hot. Cold. This is the inheritance, pale tiny faces in the gloom. Who shall be happy if not...? Not! Not! *(He reaches for the rest: it's still not there)*... And it was decreed that the sacred Empire of Images should stretch to the world's edge and beyond. And death would be no impediment. And lo! the great and willing David, at a cost of not less than the annual earnings of all the menu people of Nantes put together, defied Nature for three whole days in high stinking summer so that the blessed Martyr Marat's assassinated bodily remains might tastefully, decently and enduringly preside in person over his own funeral rites, Nature would be bettered. The body would be emptied and stuffed, the knife-wounds decorously diminished in size and stature for art's sake, the distressing skin condition masked, the unusably battered right arm that was to hold the telling steel pen cut off and replaced with one in fuller working order from the mortuary, the residual stench of natural decay perfumed to sweetness, the unheroically lolling tongue slit on four strategic sites to hold it steady... Never mind we fight wars on four fronts, never mind the British blockade shrivels supplies of food, never mind the country will soon collapse into civil and atrocious war with itself... The Empire of Images knows no nay and will be served...

(Fipple-flute cuts; drums plays on.)

PRISONER. ...Did we imagine *this* would not be remembered too? And. Built upon...?

(Drum cuts.)

PRISONER. Did Danton do this? Did any of us? For what? To make the world a better place for our class of people?

(Back-wall and downspot slowly die. The lips mutter on.)

PRISONER. ...If not. Not. If not...

(Fade to black.)

(Fade up.)

PRISONER. *(from black)* Ye still there? Of course you are...

*(Salle, cage. Strong sunlight shafts in from above, reshaping the space. The **PRISONER** stands in the cage all but naked, washing and sluicing his body with water from a metal bowl. Fade up reflected audience on back wall.)*

PRISONER. Looking back's all that's left ye, *you* spent what was left of the future long since, you have nowhere else to look save back, do ye, poor sods... *(Looks out at the dark, smiles)* For myself, and for my sins, I'm doomed to hope and chained to the present. This sixteenth day of Germinal in the Second Year of the Free Republic. *(Approaches the front bars, drying himself)* You are in my hands. Here, now. I feel you. We are the same flesh. Composed of the same atoms. Everything we have thought, everything we have tried or imagined, everything dreamt and whispered, designed, done... you will develop and perfect. Such a dish of worms we've served ye and ye'll eat 'em, every one. The free dance of capital, the human imperative. The sovereign people, the allseeing allsaying State. Owner, worker. Nation and war, people and peace. The power of the machine, the machinery of power. Me, all. The impossible and the necessary dream. The road to freedom, mined every step of the way...

*(**HENRY** trudges up, a tray in his hands. The reflected audience fades.)*

HENRY. *(muttering, angry)* This is not guards' work. Bastards.

*(The **PRISONER**'s dressing; crosses to the door to be shackled.)*

HENRY. *(shackling with double legiron)* Ye done? Yer carriage's come. Ye're to leave at the half.

*(The **PRISONER** nods, stretches, turns to gather his things.)*

HENRY. I've to cut your hair.

PRISONER. What?

HENRY. Cut your hair.

PRISONER. What for?

HENRY. Because I'm told to. I'm to lift the hair from your collar.

*(He removes the linen cloth: bowl, shears, combs, metal mirror. The **PRISONER** watches carefully.)*

HENRY. Them's the orders.

(He gestures him to sit at the table.)

PRISONER. *(slow)* I understood the Man was still in trial, witnesses to be called, evidence to be heard...

HENRY. That was yesterday. You wanna sit, friend?

(The **PRISONER** *leaves the cage, clanks slowly to the table, sits, face pale, still.* **HENRY** *combs out his back hair, sizing up the cut needed.)*

HENRY. Trial's declared over. Jury's asked to proceed to judgment. Verdict's expected within the hour. S'what they say, how would I know...?

PRISONER. If ye're cutting neck-hair, somebody knows, Henry...

HENRY. Happen.

(He shears off a hand of hair, lays it on the table. The man stares at it. The shears hover for the next slice.)

PRISONER. Poor sod.

HENRY. Maybe.

(A second cut, another hand to the table. The **PRISONER** *picks it up, examines it.)*

PRISONER. Hey.

HENRY. What?

PRISONER. Ye done this before?

HENRY. No.

PRISONER. I thought not, Don't send me out like a bloody page boy, understood?

HENRY. This is Headsman's work.

PRISONER. Nevertheless.

HENRY. It'll grow.

PRISONER. Will it?

(Silence. **HENRY** *eventually resumes the cut.)*

PRISONER. He's dead then.

HENRY. Good as.

PRISONER. Poor sod.

HENRY. Why?

PRISONER. Why?

HENRY. Ye think he's innocent?

PRISONER. No one is innocent, friend…

HENRY. …Then he's guilty. Fuck him.

(Silence.)

PRISONER. Guilty of what?

HENRY. How should I know?

PRISONER. Guilty of what?

HENRY. Living fat off the people, how 'bout that…?

PRISONER. That's most folk in britches, Henry.

HENRY. Ahunh.

(Silence. HENRY's all but finished. Holds up angled mirror.)

HENRY. Ye wanna see?

PRISONER. No.

(HENRY begins to clear away and ferry trays down the room. The PRISONER sits on in silence, hands on table, the fingers twitching as he broods.)

PRISONER. Is there word from your cousin?

HENRY. None. He'll be well abed by now.

PRISONER. And the letter…?

HENRY. No word, no problem. It's done.

(Town clock strikes the half. Silence. A brief look shared.)

PRISONER. You're an honest man, Henry. I thank ye for your trust.

(HENRY heads off with the ablutions tray.)

PRISONER. (flicking a glance at the dark) So. The farce ends. Almost time for last words… Clop across the Pont-au-Change, pass the Quai de la Mégisserie, along the Rue de la Monnaie, down the Rue Honoré to the Rue National, a wave for the terrace of the Café du

Montparnasse – Gabrielle, Louise – And... Eh voilà!... Place de la Révolution. Where all this...history began. Alpha and Omega. The first and the last. Full circle. I am here. Last words then. What shall they be? Be sure to show them my head, it's worth seeing...? Let the Committee take my head, the people already have my heart...? *(starts chuckling)* Now ye see me, now ye don't...?

(Banging at the doors again. He turns, peers at **HENRY** *talking through the grille.)*

PRISONER. *(still dealing with Last Words)*... No, I should leave with a question... *(He stands, puts his hands behind his back as if tied, gazes out across the muted throng.)* WHO SHALL BE HAPPY...? IF...? WHO SHALL BE HAPPY, IF NOT...? IF *NOT*...?

*(***HENRY*** up the room sharpish, fiddling a length of rope from his pocket.)*

HENRY. You're to be readied, the Guards're on their way... Your cart's stood by.

(He wraps the rope around the **PRISONER***'s wrists, still behind his back, secures them.)*

PRISONER. *(carefully)* Cart, Henry?

HENRY. Cart, carriage...

(In the silence, the sound of hooves, wheels on courtyard cobble nearby.)

PRISONER. So is there. A verdict through?

HENRY. *(not looking)* Guilty. All charges.

(He tugs at the second anklet. Stands. Eyes meet.)

HENRY. Ye right, are ye?

PRISONER. I'm searching a question, Henry. Have to find it.

HENRY. It'll have to wait. *(Draws a leather hood from his pocket)* Ye're to leave as ye came...

(Silence.)

PRISONER. *(staring at it)* In our ends lie our beginnings...?

HENRY. What?

PRISONER. Last words.

HENRY. Game's over. *(prepares the hood)* Orders.

*(Silence. The **PRISONER** shuffles to the stool, sits, his back to the guard. **HENRY** quietly moves in behind him.)*

PRISONER. I see.

*(**HENRY** bags the head, draws the cords, ties them.)*

HENRY. Ye breathin'?

*(Close shot of the hooded face. Only the lips, nostrils and chin are darkly visible, beyond the air-slit provided at the mouth. He nods. **HENRY** leaves the table area, gathering up his gear and belongings. A tight spot frames the **PRISONER**'s hooded face, the vent, the barely seen mouth behind it.)*

PRISONER. *(a whisper)* I'm sixteen. I'm in Rheims. I'm standing in a long line of dignitaries clutching their cards of invitation outside the Cathedral. My clothes are borrowed, the money for the journey stolen, I have no card but I will go through, I will see the young Louis anointed King, let him stop me who dare. The town police keep back the crowds. There are cheers for the queuing worthies, I find myself...waving acknowledgment. Just ahead, a clamour of beggars has wormed a way through the barricades and onto the steps of the West Door. Worthy coins appear on cue to soothe their noise, I fumble for a spare ten-sous piece, heart thumping I'll be found out... *(Long silence. Remote sounds of fists on doors down the room.)* One year ago. A day or so

After.

After.

My Gabrielle. Birthing a dead

daughter...

Died...

(*Silence.*)

And I had.

Detained in Belgium.

Back too late. Dug up

her corpse...

Detained in Belgium, did ye say... ?

Service to the Revolution the highest law

implied...? Pull the other

one, my friend, it plays

a tolerable version of

Ça Ira. In Belgium ye were

Looking out for yourself.

Doing deals, securing

Your loot, covering your tracks,

Saving France of course

And fucking

Everything in skirts

That moved.

(*Silence.*)

PRISONER. And knew. All

Along. She was like

To die.

With this one...

(*Silence. The lips move on, soundless.* **HENRY**'s *at the door, standing the* **PRISONER**'s *escorts by; eventually begins the trudge back towards the table.*)

PRISONER. No one is innocent. Living's a guilty business...

HENRY. (*from distance*) Let's go.

PRISONER. *(fast, urgent)...* Heart thumping I'll be found out. A beggar reaches for my ten-sous piece, his thick hand snaps around my wrist, I cannot shake the bugger, the tocsin swells, I'll miss the King... The beggar speaks: Ask him a question. Ask him a question. Come back and tell me what he says. Ask him...

*(***HENRY***'s arrived. Waits, frowning, in the growing silence.)*

HENRY. Let's go.

PRISONER. *(simply)* Who shall be happy, if not everyone?

*(Silence. ***HENRY*** taps the ***PRISONER***'s shoulder, helps him up.)*

PRISONER. Henry.

HENRY. What?

PRISONER. I'll say goodbye.

HENRY. Aye.

*(He leads him out; scans the room; gathers a few remaining odds and ends; places then on or by the table for off. Picks up a lamp, lays it on a stool. Sits on the other stool, takes out watch, ring and purse of money, lays them out. The greatcoat joins them. He takes out his pipe. Can't find his flint. Reaches for his musket. Removes the furled letter from the barrel. Tapers it to the lamp. Lights his pipe. Fipple flute and drum: Ça Ira. Salle, cage. Flute out; drum on alone. ***HENRY*** gathers his gear, trudges off. The back-wall comes to life again: the audience is left with itself. Fast fade to black.)*

End

PROVISIONAL PROP LIST

Musket (Henry)
Tray
Food (meat & wine)
Watch (Prisoner)
Keys (to cage & leg iron)
Chain & leg iron
Bowl
Razor
Metal Mirror
Towel
Tray
Money (sous)
Flask (containing brand) (Henry)
Clay Pipe (Henry)
Pipe Tobacco
Flint
Bar of soap
Draw Purse
Gold Wedding Ring (Prisoner)
Letter (Danton to Wife)
Fipple Flute
Wig (Robespierre)
Playing Cards (Henry)
Large Handkerchief
Black Bread
Few Oats Cheese
Green Potato
Knapsack (Henry)
Bottle of wine
Battered tin cups x 2
Handkerchief (Prisoner)
Large Metal Bowl
2nd Metal Bowl
Linen cloth
Bowl (for hair cutting)
Shears
Comb

Length of Rope (for tying hands)
Leather Hood with draw cord
Cage
Chaise Longue
Chair
Lamp
Card Table
Stool
Straw
Shattered Chandelier
Ancient Wingchair (one leg missing)
Lumber & Rubble

www.ingramcontent.com/pod-product-compliance
Lightning Source LLC
Chambersburg PA
CBHW070421120726
47909CB00005B/1740